Disney
FROZEN
A Year with
Elsa & Anna
(and Olaf, too!)

written by Marie

studio fun
A READER'S DIGEST COMPANY

White Plains, New York · Montréal, Québec · Bath, United Kingdom

A Note from the Author

Nestled in the heart of a frosty fjord is the best kingdom of them all—Arendelle! What makes it the best? The spectacular mountains? The glittering bay? The way the air smells so delicately of fish? Nope. It's the people, especially Queen Elsa and Princess Anna! I'm biased, I admit, because I've studied Arendelle my whole life. And I finally got to spend some time there!

My name's Marie, and my family and I spent a year in Arendelle while my father made a new bell for the town square. That's harder than you might think. Bell makers are always trying for a *ding-dong*, but if they're not careful they get a *dong-ding*. But not my dad! He always gets it right.

Can you believe how pretty this scrapbook turned out?

I've created this scrapbook to share my wonderful insider experiences with you. By the way, I bet you're seeing some notes here and there. Sometimes I get so excited I forget stuff the first time around. (Sometimes I just can't help myself! Like here.) And I wouldn't want you to miss a thing!

Your enthusiastic Arendelle expert,

Marie

Arendelle is famed for its beauty and wonderful weather. But you have to love snow (seriously, that's a double-must). See the painting below? It was painted in October last year. By December, everyone in that first row of houses had to stay with people in the second row—because they couldn't get in their own front doors!

When summer finally arrives, the weather is warm enough to melt Olaf in ten seconds—that is, if he weren't magic! Good thing the ice harvesters go high into the mountains, braving the wilds for ice to keep everyone's icebox cold. Without them, nobody could keep food fresh, and all the lemonade would be warm. (Yuck!)

If you ever decide to visit, make sure to have someone show you around. If I were still there, I'd be happy to do it, though some people don't appreciate the level of detail I get into. Isn't everyone curious about Arendelle's average rainfall on weekends in May?

Here's Elsa's birth announcement. The town printer made tons of these. The king and queen kept all the leftovers and Elsa gave me this one to keep!

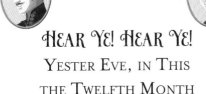

HEAR YE! HEAR YE!
YESTER EVE, IN THIS THE TWELFTH MONTH

King Agnarr and Queen Iduna were delivered of a royal princess at Arendelle Castle! The princess, a flaxen-haired beauty, weighing seven pounds, will bear the esteemed moniker of Elsa. Princess Elsa, all hail her name, was born amidst the splendiloquent luminosities of the aurora borealis. Her birth was accompanied by an unanticipated meteorological phenomenon that blanketed the village in delicate crystals of ice.

Both mother and child are well and taking their repose.

MEET ANNA, NOT JUST A BABY SISTER:

Princess Anna is adventurous and full of energy! She loves making friends—even with painted portraits if she has to—and stands up for those she loves with all her courage, especially Elsa. If it weren't for Anna's optimistic heart, Arendelle would be a very different place. Sometimes, though, she's so enthusiastic that she acts before she thinks, and every so often that gets her a bit stuck. Or makes her slip. Or trip. Good thing she knows how to pick herself up!

Anna's birthday is on the summer solstice!

Weather: Chance of Snow: 60%
Chance of Sun: 75–80%
Chance of this weather report being accurate: 7%

TWO CENTS

PRINCESS PRESENTED TO THE PEOPLE!

Today marks the first appearance of King Agnarr and Queen Iduna since the birth of their second daughter, Anna, during the summer solstice.

The royal couple appeared on the balcony overlooking the courtyard to present the days-old princess to the public. Sources close to the palace say that Princess Anna favors her mother, but this reporter glimpsed a particularly strong chin reminiscent of the king himself.

The adorable royal baby has strawberry-blonde hair, green eyes, and some say a smattering of freckles. She was swaddled in an heirloom receiving blanket first donned by her sister, Elsa. The king and queen were accompanied by the elder princess, who is now toddling on chubby legs.

Elsa and Anna aren't afraid to be themselves, and
neither are their friends. See this portrait? Everyone
knows Olaf, but did you know Sven is the reindeer? And
Kristoff is just beside Anna. Kristoff and Sven are good
friends—Sven is the handsome one. I can't believe they all
sat still long enough to be painted!

Check out my
portrait of
Elsa & Anna!

SPRING

MAR

Forest
Walk

APRIL

Star-
Gazing
with
Olaf

Picnic
with
Anna
& Elsa

MAY

Flower Show →

Trail
Cleanup
Day

Oaken's Spring
Blowout!

Baby
Reindeer?

SPRING HAS SPRUNG!

Spring in Arendelle was magnificent! Elsa decided to do something special to mark the beginning of the season. At sunrise on the very first day of spring, in the castle courtyard, Elsa used her powers to create a giant ice sculpture! She's done this a few times before, and no one ever knows just what the sculpture will be.

This time, Elsa created a sculpture of Princess Anna—and we finally saw what the princess looks like standing still! Over the next few days, the sculpture melted. I hope Anna didn't mind. But without some ice-melting, it wouldn't be spring, would it?

Elsa got lots of suggestions. She let me have these lists for my scrapbook!

Olaf's Ice Sculpture Ideas:
(Elsa, he told me to write this! A.)
• A carrot
• Twigs
• A warm hug
(Elsa, is this one even possible?)

Anna's Ice Sculpture Ideas:
(Elsa, thought you'd appreciate some help!)

• Kristoff (his business IS ice!)

• Olaf (the stick arms might be tricky)

• Sven (never mind, the antlers would be a nightmare!)

• Hans (who wouldn't enjoy watching him melt?)

I agree with Anna! Olaf would look great as an ice sculpture!

Kristoff:
Anna!

Looks like Elsa liked Kristoff's idea best!

No one makes better ice sculptures than Elsa!

ARENDELLE SPRING TRADITIONS

As the days warmed, crocuses were the first flowers to push their colorful petals through the soft soil. Did you know that the crocus is the official flower of Arendelle? It's even featured on the banners all around town!

In Arendelle, they take flowers very seriously. I mean, as seriously as you *can* take flowers. Every year, the village hosts a flower show. The Arendelle Spring Flower Show is world famous, and people come from far and wide to see the beautiful arrangements. Every year there is a contest to see who can make the most creative arrangement. This year's theme was "Bountiful Blooms." I decided to enter the contest for fun!

If flowers make you sneeze, there's something else they take really seriously in Arendelle: reindeer. There's a big competition with prizes for herding, log pulling, even antler decorating!

The Kingdom
of Arendelle Presents
Its 47th Annual

SPRING FLOWER SHOW

BOUNTIFUL BLOOMS

April 27th–May 7th
in the Arendelle
Castle Courtyard

Don't miss the contest for
Best Flower Arrangement
judged by Queen Elsa and
Princess Anna!

A few days before the contest, I hiked to the mountain meadows to pick flowers for my arrangement. Then, I spotted something unusual: A tiny mountain of purple and pink flowers hopping across the fields. It was Olaf! He was covered in crocuses.

"I'm entering the contest!" he said.

"It's a flower show, not a fashion show," I joked.

Olaf glanced down at himself. "That's just how I carry them," he giggled. "They even stay fresh!"

After the judging, Elsa and Anna announced three winners: Norvald the Millner for his "Fresh as a Daisy," Letty Pedersen for her "Watering Can in Bloom," and me(!) for my "Lots of Lilies" arrangement. Olaf's creation, called "Stick with Me," was so unique that he received an honorable mention!

By the end of the day Olaf was tuckered out. I'm not surprised. He almost left an arm behind on his way home.

Spring Trail Cleanup

Every spring, Queen Elsa, Princess Anna, and their friends hike into the mountains to clean up the trails. This year, Kristoff decided to stay behind for some much-needed reindeer spring-cleaning. You'd think Sven could clean himself, but he *definitely* has some hard-to-reach places!

Happy to volunteer, I hiked up with them. Cleanup might not sound like a good time, but trust me, with Anna and Elsa EVERYTHING is a good time. Besides, it gave me a chance to get to know Olaf better, too!

As we picked up dead branches and dry leaves, I made up a poem. Before long, I had written a masterpiece! There is nothing like fresh air and good friends to get the creative juices flowing!

An instant classic!

Marie's Cleanup Poem

Cleaning, cleaning
over the mountain range.
I aim to clean
until things gleam
and that will never change.

Cleaning, cleaning
shoo away the bugs.
Pick up the sticks
we'll finish quick
and follow with warm hugs.

When we reached the summit of the mountain, Oaken was waiting with a picnic!

"You must be hungry, ja?" he said.

There was something about being around Oaken that made us all want to strike deals with each other. Anna agreed to eat two sandwiches if Elsa tried the cabbage salad. I got the best deal—if I ate some pudding, Oaken would clean up after us. And I thought *he* was a master negotiator! One thing is for sure—Oaken is a great cook. I jotted down his family recipe for lutefisk. Maybe I will try making it for my family back home.

Oaken's Own Lutefisk-Making Instructions
(transcribed by Marie!)

1. Build a wooden drying frame. If you need help, ask Kristoff!
2. Gather your fresh cod. Catch it yourself, but if that doesn't work out, it's available at Oaken's.
3. Lay the cod on the frame. Wait for wind and sun to dry the cod.
4. Store carefully (for up to several years, ja? says Oaken).
5. When ready to eat, soak dry fish in mixture of water and lye.
6. Wash fish, then steam or oven bake until cooked (make sure you make enough for Oaken!)
7. Eat!

Everyone here loves
this stuff!

No one noticed it was late until it was time to walk back to the village. It was getting dark and it seemed like we were going to have to spend the night on the mountain. Elsa wasn't worried. She raised her arms and snowflakes began to whirl around her. She shaped them into an enormous icy slide that stretched down to the valley. It was incredible!

I didn't ever bring a coat!

I started wondering what it would be like to use ice slides to get everywhere, all the time. Ice slide from castle to market, ice slide to the valley, ice slide to the skating pond! Maybe I'll suggest them to Elsa!

In no time, we reached the bottom of the mountain. It's one day of cleaning I'll never forget!

Hoo Hoo!
BIG Spring Blowout!
OAKEN'S
Refreshing
Lemonade

Sorry, we can't reveal the royal identity of the person here who clearly loves Oaken's *Refreshing* Lemonade!

Hint: She doesn't need ice cubes to cool off her delicious *Refreshing* Lemonade!

Oh, Baby!

Later in the spring, there was some exciting news in the town square. Anna and Elsa were called to the royal stables.

A new baby reindeer had been born in the early morning hours! The sisters and Olaf were so excited they danced in circles. Olaf was lucky he didn't lose both arms with all the joyful twirling!

Like any baby, the reindeer needed a name, and the sisters decided to invite everyone in Arendelle to make suggestions. An official sign was posted in the square, and word spread quickly. Everyone had an idea, and I think you can spot Olaf's!

IT'S A BOY!

SUGGEST A NAME FOR
THE NEWEST REINDEER
IN THE ROYAL STABLES!

Bjorn

Snuggles

Rolf

Lars

Spot

Waffle

Mr. Caribou

Rudolph

Sardine Wigglebutt

Carrot

These are what baby reindeer tracks look like!

I was posting a name suggestion on the list in town when I overheard that the baby reindeer had gone missing. Nobody could find him. Anna and Elsa sprang into action and followed tiny hoofprints to a small hole in the stable fence. The tracks led deep into the woods. This meant only one thing: an expedition was in order. I hurried to tag along!

We went straight to Oaken for supplies. Anna and Elsa grabbed a length of rope and some lingonberry-infused water—searching is thirsty work! It can also leave a girl hungry, so we were all eyeing the boxes of fresh Reindeer-Tracks Trail Mix (an Oaken original, of course).

"How about some new snowshoes too, ja?" Oaken said. "Emergency discount!"

Anna and Elsa couldn't resist. At the very least, they could save them for the first snowfall (which in Arendelle comes sooner than you think).

Hours up the trail, we heard a sound. But it wasn't so reindeer-ish as snowman-ish. It was Olaf!

"Over here!" he said, waving his arms frantically at the top of a cliff. As we got closer, we heard *another* sound— definitely hooves! The baby reindeer was on a ledge below.

"Don't worry, little guy," Elsa said to him. She's not just good with ice, but with animals, too.

Elsa made a snow ramp and tried to lure the reindeer up with Olaf's nose, but the ramp was too slippery and he kept sliding down. Anna slid down, too, to try to help him up, but at that point the little one was too scared to budge.

Then Anna had an amazing idea: "Let's use the snowshoes! We can put them on his feet, and I'll push him up!" Her plan worked perfectly. Soon he was back in the stable, safe and sound.

Perfect fit!

The next day, Anna and Elsa gave the little reindeer a beautiful collar embroidered with his new name. Can you guess what name they chose? *Psst*, I'll give you a hint—not Carrot, not Waffle (sniff, sniff), and certainly not Sardine Wigglebutt!

Elsa announced the reindeer's name: Lars. It's a wonderful name, but I still call him Waffle for short.

Keep an eye on your nose, Olaf!

SUMMER

JUNE

Help Dad
Pick Bell
Design

Anna's
Birthd

JULY

Beach
Day!

Read
About
Zaria

AUGUST

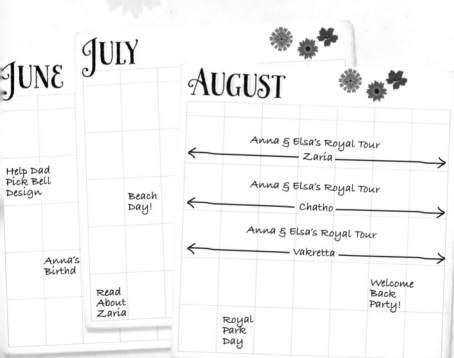

Anna & Elsa's Royal Tour
← Zaria →

Anna & Elsa's Royal Tour
← Chatho →

Anna & Elsa's Royal Tour
← Vakretta →

Welcome
Back
Party!

Royal
Park
Day

Happy Birthday, Anna!

Summer is known for long days, warm sunshine, mosquitoes.... In Arendelle, the start of summer is known for something else—Princess Anna's birthday! This year, Queen Elsa planned a supersized surprise party. She wanted everything to be perfect, right down to the last glittering dollop of cake frosting.

She made at least ten different cake toppers before choosing this one!

Speaking of cake…Olaf named himself the official cake tester—someone had to make sure it was fit for a princess! He was so enthusiastic, he got his mouth full of icing and he thought it tasted good! At that point, Elsa decided to appoint him official icing design consultant. Olaf loved that new job, too.

Elsa woke Anna early in the morning. Every part of Anna buzzed with excitement—even her hair!

That's one extraordinary case of bed head!

Elsa couldn't wait to show Anna the surprises she had planned, but she wasn't feeling quite right. Elsa had the sniffles. When she sneezed, the strangest thing happened—tiny snowmen dropped out of thin air. I guess her magic powers were catching cold, too! Not to be confused with Olaf, these snowmen are called snowgies. Cute, right? WRONG! Snowgies are trouble!

They are pretty cute!

Elsa didn't notice the snowgies as they hurried out of sight. She was too eager to reveal Anna's first birthday surprise—a beautiful new dress from Anna's favorite shop in Arendelle. Then Elsa added her own special touch— delicate icy sparkles along the edge!

Elsa handed Anna one end of a piece of string and told her to follow it. The string led through the castle and the castle grounds! Elsa went all-out with gifts. Turn the page to see my favorites!

I think green is Anna's color! It really brings out her eyes!

Look at the dress Elsa conjured for herself! Amazing!

ANNA'S GIFT GALLERY

A suit of armor made an excellent jewelry box to hold a pretty bracelet.

Is that a cuckoo clock? No! It's an Olaf clock!

Now Anna can talk to a picture of herself and all her friends!

Scavenger hunting is hungry work. Birthday picnic!

Long staircases are no match for Elsa's birthday bike tour!

Only Kristoff was strong enough to deliver the cake.

Meanwhile, Elsa kept sneezing…and making more snowgies! They got into everything—including the party decorations. Kristoff and Olaf tried to round them up, but that was easier said than done. Olaf wasn't much help— he was too distracted meeting all his new little brothers.

By the time Elsa brought Anna to the courtyard for her last surprise, the snowgies had all but taken over! Brilliantly, Kristoff and Olaf turned them into part of the decorations, an adorable touch of winter in summer. They were the biggest surprise of the day…almost. Kristoff *finally* told Anna he loves her!

Romance makes the best gift! xoxo

Buttercream frosting!
Yum!

What happened to the snowgies, you ask? They went to live with Marshmallow at Elsa's ice palace. Olaf is still trying to give them all names. He's been at it for months!

Can you imagine having that many brothers?

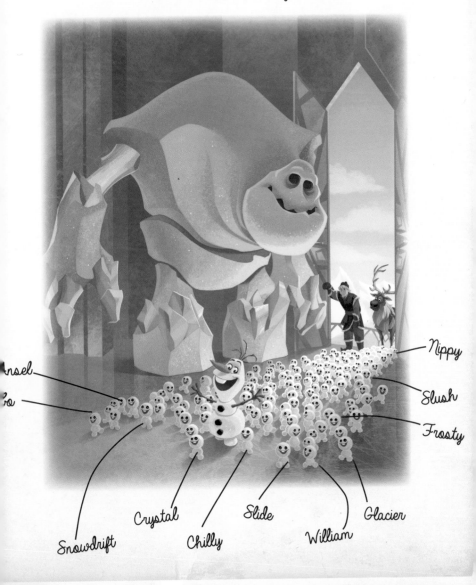

WANDERING OAKEN'S

SUN BALM

Oaken says:

Half off a sun balm of my own invention, ja?

ALL NATURAL
COMPLETELY SAFE

CAUTION: Side effects may or may not include hiccups, freckles, sneezing, long eyelashes, daydreaming, or any combination of the aforementioned.
Use as directed.

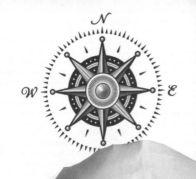

The Royal Tour

Summer is a great time to travel. This year, Princess Anna and Queen Elsa went on a royal tour, which is just a fancy way of saying they visited kings and queens of other lands. It was their first time away from Arendelle! While they were away, things were definitely less fun around here, but I spent that time working on this book and collecting odds and ends to put inside. I also spent *a lot* of time in Oaken's sauna! Finally, Anna and Elsa returned and told everyone about their trip.

Anna gave me her ticket and packing list for my scrapbook!

Packing list

Me
✓ Chocolate candy
✓ Dresses and stuff
✓ Chocolate cake
✓ Other cake
✓ Cake
  Bicycle
✓ Nightgown
  Postcards & stamps

Elsa
✓ Oaken's Sun Balm

ROUND-TRIP TICKET

PASSENGER NAME
Princess Anna

CABIN
Royal Suite

Can you guess who was as green on the HMS *Arendelle* as Anna's dress? The captain! I guess seasickness even strikes old-timers. Elsa quickly dug out a bottle of Oaken's Ocean Remedy. Two drops under his tongue and he was so thankful he let her try steering the ship! The first stop was the kingdom of Zaria where the sisters were welcomed by Queen Renalia and King Stebor. They were delighted to have visitors and showed

Elsa and Anna their beautiful gardens. The sisters saw exotic plants—one flower was even Olaf shaped!

One night the king and queen threw a party in Anna's and Elsa's honor and invited all the villagers. The dances were not familiar to the princess, but Anna made up for her lack of knowledge with sheer enthusiasm. Her dance steps were so distinctive, people started copying them! They even named a new dance move after her: the Anna of Arendelle Quadruple-Step! After dancing with the Duke of Wesselton at Elsa's coronation, Anna proved she could dance with anyone.

Next stop was the kingdom of Chatho, ruled by Queen Colisa. She welcomed Elsa and Anna with open arms, eager to show them one of Chatho's well-known sights—its amazing rain forest.

The spectacular forest captivated Anna and Elsa. Anna's highlight was meeting a gentle creature called a sloth. Sloths might be slow moving, but don't call them lazy—they get it all done, it just...takes...a long...time! And they're very friendly—one reached out to shake hands, er, claws, with the princess.

Before they left, the sisters were also lucky enough to see Chatho's collection of artifacts from all over the world. Elsa got lots of ideas for future ice sculptures, and even made one for a temporary display in Chatho's museum!

Anna loved the jade lion!

The final stop was Vakretta, but there was no one to meet the sisters. The streets were abandoned. Then Elsa and Anna realized it was extraordinarily hot! Sure enough, the townsfolk were weathering the heat wave by hiding inside their homes. Too bad Kristoff wasn't there—his business would have been booming!

Elsa knew how to help. She lifted her arms and summoned frosty magic. Cold air settled overhead and delicate snowflakes fell from the sky. The townspeople couldn't believe their eyes! Anna and Elsa served everyone mugs of cold lemonade, chilled with ice cubes created by the queen herself—talk about a royal treat! It was the perfect end to the tour.

Postcards from the Royal Tour!

VAKRETTA

CHATHO

ZARIA

A Day for the Children

Royal Park Day is another Arendelle summer tradition. Queen Elsa and Princess Anna invite the village children for a picnic on the castle grounds. Everyone in the castle pitches in to prepare, including Olaf!

"I might be baking cookies, but they're making me slimmer!" he said, as he started to melt near the oven. Elsa quickly fixed him up and put him on lemonade duty instead. There is nothing like a snowman to keep a pitcher of lemonade cool!

Look who's un-bee-lievably happy!

In the castle gardens, Elsa told fairy tales beneath
a large willow tree, and showed her audience how to wish
on dandelion fuzz. I wished for summer to go on forever,
but I think one kid asked for an early winter. Maybe
they'll cancel each other out!

Anna led an adventurous group on a butterfly hunt.
One landed on my nose, and I named it Flutter right
before it flew away. I guess I had a pet butterfly for
a whole ten seconds!

The children must have had fun, because the next day
a stack of thank-you notes arrived at the castle. Anna and
Elsa got so many, they let me have some for my scrapbook!

Dear Anna & Elsa,

I was so happy to visit Arendelle castle for Royal Park Day. Thank you for inviting me. I have a question I forgot to ask you. Is Olaf's nose a real carrot? My brother says yes, but I don't think so.

Best wishes,

Dear Queen Elsa & Princess Anna,

Thank you so much for inviting me to the castle! I had the best time. My favorite part was wishing on the dandelion! I wished for a tail. I also picked a flower from the garden to keep forever. I hope you don't mind.

Hi Princess Anna & Queen Elsa!

I really really really really really really really had a great time at the castle! My mom says I should thank you a lot. So here goes. Thank you, thank you, thank you, thank you, thank you, thank you, thank you, thank you, thank you, thank you, thank you!

Yours Truly,
Einar

Dear Queen Elsa and Princess Anna,

Royal Park Day is my favorite day of the year. I love to play in the castle gardens. Thank you so much for hosting us!

By the way, I'm your number one fan!

Sincerely,
Marie

The Perfect Summer Day (According to Olaf!)

Most people enjoy summer, but I know someone who takes it to the extreme—the most summer-loving snowman of them all…Olaf! Since Elsa gave him his own personal flurry, he can happily bask in the noonday sun. Most snowmen don't even know that summer *exists*. It's probably good they don't—there would be so many snowmen about, summer would look just like winter!

Olaf was excited to tell me his suggestions for creating the most perfect summer day ever. First, start with a lazy boat ride through a fjord. The gentle rocking of the waves is like a dream—unless you get seasick! Don't forget to bring Oaken's Ocean Remedy—just in case.

Captain Olaf on deck. All hands at ease!

What's the destination? Where else, but a stunning beach! Take a dip—that is, if you feel like hitching up your skirt to brave the crisp Arendelle waters. Water too cold for you? Chill out on a blanket instead, but make sure you are covered in Wandering Oaken's Sun Balm. You don't want to burn!

(This is especially important if you are Elsa!)

While on the beach, why not make a sand angel? If you've heard of snow angels, sand angels are almost the same—just more gritty than frosty. Follow Olaf's simple steps:

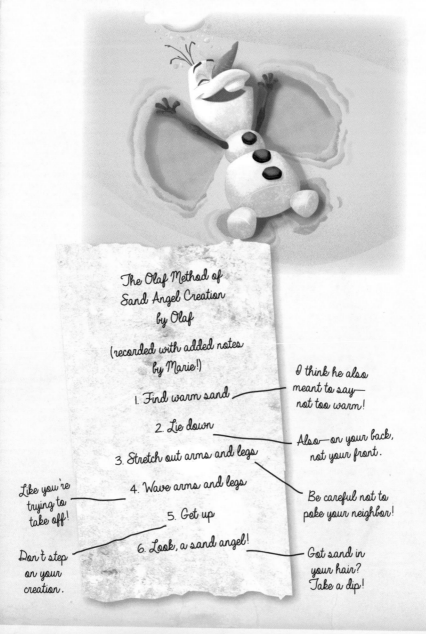

The Olaf Method of
Sand Angel Creation
by Olaf

(recorded with added notes
by Marie!)

1. Find warm sand

I think he also meant to say— not too warm!

2. Lie down

Also—on your back, not your front.

3. Stretch out arms and legs

4. Wave arms and legs

Like you're trying to take off!

Be careful not to poke your neighbor!

5. Get up

6. Look, a sand angel!

Don't step on your creation.

Got sand in your hair? Take a dip!

Tuckered out from all that arm flapping? Olaf suggests a construction project, beach style! Sculpt your friends, or build a castle just like the one you live in. Anna and Elsa are so good at sand-castle building that they even use driftwood to make little pieces of furniture for the courtyard!

For your summer day grand finale, Olaf recommends...an island party! It's the most festive way to celebrate the summer, partly because it comes with unique outfits—grass skirts and flower necklaces! Note: If your reindeer refuses to wear a grass skirt, just decorate his antlers with flowers.

The one thing you just can't have an island party without? Friends. Olaf recommends inviting everyone you know—even people you don't. The more the merrier, Olaf says. There's no better ending to a perfect summer day—take it from Arendelle's expert resident snowman.

This entry is Olaf-approved!

Autumn

September

Mom's Birthday!

Har Fest

Ask Gerda Debut!

October

Go Apple Picking!

November

Bake Apple Pies

Eat Apple Pies

Bake More Pies

Press Fall Leaves

Help Dad Make Bell Mold

Troll-Sitting for Beginners
(As told to Marie by Anna and Kristoff)

Fall is a dreamy season, especially in Arendelle. Many things happen just like they do at home, like leaves drifting to the ground in piles perfect to jump into. But some things are different. This year there was a special gathering of the trolls. Bulda and Grand Pabbie went and needed someone to babysit for the night. That's right, babysit the...troll babies! They asked Kristoff, who invited Anna because he knew she'd be excited. And she was, but nervous, too.

"How much trouble can we get from some baby rocks?" he said, laughing.

Famous last words, Kristoff!

When the babysitters arrived, Bulda informed them that it was almost the babies' bedtime. "Beforehand, the babies might need a meal of smashed berries," she said, "and, likely, a nappy change!"

By the way...trolls use only the strongest and biggest Arendelle maple leaves for nappies. You sure don't want them ripping when the babies are playing and tumbling all over the place! And the moment Bulda and Grand Pabbie were out of sight, that's exactly what the baby trolls did. Working together, they escaped their pen and rolled off in all directions!

Anna and Kristoff scrambled around trying to catch them, but you'd be surprised how fast troll babies are. Even though holding one is like carrying a (very) heavy rock, if you put it down the baby will disappear like quicksand.

The babysitters had to calm down the trolls somehow. They tried feeding them. No luck. Kristoff was brave enough to check their nappies—still fresh and clean! And the babies certainly weren't sleepy—they were climbing trees and scaling a cliff! Anna and Kristoff didn't know what to do. Then a merry voice called to them—it was Olaf! He was a welcome sight.

Even though Elsa
hasn't spent as much time
around trolls as Anna and
Kristoff, she still had
a feeling they might have
their hands full. So she
sent everyone's favorite
snowman—who, as always,
was an immediate star. The
trolls were soon climbing
all over Olaf!

Whoops!

Anna ran to greet Olaf, tripped, and fell face-first into the basket of smashed-berry troll baby food. When she got up, she looked like she'd put on a purple beauty mask! (Actually, I hear they're excellent for your skin…I'm wearing one as I write this.)

But just when Anna thought things had hit rock bottom—so to speak—all the troll babies started licking her face!

She told me it was like getting a facial massage with handfuls of rough pebbles. *Ouch!* Full of smashed berries, the troll babies *finally* rested, happily.

But then they started to, er... how do I put this? Smell, a bit. Okay, a lot! "Leaf-changing time!" said Kristoff, pointing to their nappies. Anna gathered fresh leaves, then Kristoff rolled up his sleeves and got to work.

He's going to make a great dad someday!

"I think they're finally getting sleepy," whispered Anna, once the babies were all cleaned up. The troll babies could barely keep their eyes open.

Kristoff grabbed his lute and played a sweet lullaby. "They're dropping like rocks!" giggled Anna. Kristoff told me and Anna that he'd been preparing the song for weeks, but she was pretty sure he made it up on the spot— which is even more impressive!

By the time Bulda and Grand Pabbie came back, it was as quiet and peaceful as a snow cave. Proud of their accomplishment, Anna and Kristoff pretended it had been easy. But then Pabbie noticed some berry juice on Anna's cheek. Was he about to call their bluff?

Instead, he smiled. "Berry juice on the face, eh? Excellent way to get the children to eat. How did you come up with that idea?"

Anna had a great answer: "Guess I just fell right into it!"

This fall, a castle servant named Gerda started an advice column! So far, it's very popular!

Ask Gerda

Hello, Citizens of Arendelle!
Have a Dilemma?
Direct Your Questions to Gerda,
in Care of Arendelle Castle, and
She Will Be Happy to Write
Back with Her Advice.

Dear Kristoff,
Thank you for writing!
To answer your question, I think the young lady in question very much enjoys your company and is looking forward to many more adventures with you and your reindeer.
Sincerely, Gerda

Dear Liesel,
I am so glad to get a letter from you! Last time I saw Olaf, he definitely had both his arms. But he might have lost one since then, and that twig you found might be it!
Sincerely, Gerda

The Leaves Are Falling!
It's Time to Celebrate at the Annual Arendelle

HARVEST
FESTIVAL AND FEAST

Saturday, September 20th
Dawn till Dusk
Farmer Boberg's Back Field
(*Not* the swamp!)

Bring:
- Pumpkin for Carving
- Knife, Fork, and Plate for Feasting
- Blanket for Stargazing
- Loved Ones for Squeezing

LOOKING FORWARD
TO SEEING YOU!

As I quickly learned, there was lots of preparation for the Harvest Festival—bunads were embroidered, meatballs were rolled, and gløgg was brewed. But most important of all was harvesting the pumpkins. We needed them for the pumpkin judging. Followed by pumpkin carving. Followed by pumpkin cooking. Followed by, you guessed it...pumpkin eating!

The townspeople were thrilled that Elsa, Anna, and Kristoff helped with the pumpkin harvest—especially Kristoff, because he's so strong. He was ripping them off the vines like berries! Olaf was pretty sure someone said they were going to a pumpkin man—making contest. I think he made a new friend. Literally!

Practicing for winter!

Events

9:00   Opening Flag Parade and Dance
9:30   Fjord Horse Show
10:15 Ice Ax Juggling
11:30 Smørrebrød Picnic
12:30 Halling Dance Competition
13:00 Meatball Toss
13:30 Salmon Pickling Workshop
14:00 Log-Carrying Contest
15:00 Biggest Pumpkin Judging
15:15 Quickest Pumpkin-Carving Contest
15:30 Tastiest Pumpkin-Cooking Contest
15:45 Pumpkin-Eating Competition
16:00 Gløgg-Chugging Contest
17:00 Harvest Feast
18:30 Bonfire Sing-along
20:00 Stargazing Workshop

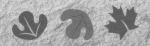

After the ice axes had been juggled, logs carried, meatballs tossed, and gløgg completely chugged, it was time to feast!

We made a special spot at the table so that Elsa, Anna, and Kristoff could join us. We tried to fit Sven, too, but he accidentally tipped over a table. We ended up putting him outside with a reindeer-sized helping of pumpkin. I think he just ended up eating grass, though. Good thing Farmer Boberg hadn't cut it for a while!

Elsa, Anna, and Kristoff had an awesome time at the feast. By the time Kristoff had finished his third hot chocolate, he was breaking into song—just in time for the bonfire sing-along!

When the autumn leaves were finished falling and the weather grew cold, everyone eagerly awaited the arrival of the most magical season of all—winter! There's nothing like cozily enjoying a crackling fire in the fireplace with a good book and a great friend.

Where I come from, we're lucky if we get a few *days* of snow, let alone several months. I glued my eyes to the windows for the very first snowflakes to fall. This year, they came early—just for me! Everyone knew that meant it would be a truly magical winter season—and a great ice harvest for Kristoff and his ice-harvesting friends!

WINTER

JANUARY

Happy
New
Year!

Help Dad
Hang Bell

DECEM

Learn to
Skate!

Elsa's
Birthday!

FEBRUARY

Winter Games

Northern Lights

Pack up
House
(Boo!)

HAPPY BIRTHDAY, ELSA!

Winter! It is what Arendelle is known for. Once the temperature started dropping and the flakes started falling, it was time for everyone to grab their ice skates and run to the lake, or snowshoe to an alpine peak for a sled race, or have a snowball fight with friends (followed by hot cocoa drinking, of course!).

Winter brings more than just cold and snowflakes, though. It's a season of celebration. Arendellians start with a big one—Elsa's birthday!

On the winter solstice, everyone feels the warm touch of the queen's heart, for instead of receiving gifts, Elsa gives them to all the children. She spends weeks going over long lists of names to make sure everyone gets something special. Then she delivers them herself, with Kristoff, Anna, and Olaf's help.

This year, Anna made something very special for Elsa—something that they both remember so fondly from their childhood...krumkake!

What are krumkake, you ask (besides a funny word)? They are scrumptious waffle cookies. Arendelle is home to one of the oldest recipes in the world! Legend says it was written hundreds of years ago by our very first queen, but no one can be certain. Many people say Queen Elsa bears a striking resemblance to her great-great-great-great-great-grandmother. Perhaps that is where her love for the cookie comes from.

Great-great-great-great-great-grandma would be proud.

My Chat with Anna and Elsa!

After seeing how close Anna and Elsa are as sisters, I wanted to know more about them. I don't have a sister (been asking for one for years), so it was fun to learn about their favorite sister memory of the year.

ELSA: One of my favorite sister memories? Most likely our impromptu slumber party.

MARIE: Impromptu?

ELSA: Yes, totally unplanned. I was asleep, in fact, happily dreaming of dessert—about to make a honey cone, and eat it! And then...I heard Anna's voice!

ANNA: Listen, I know that sounds rude, but I had been awake for hours. Like literally, four hours! Elsa was grumpy at first, so I grabbed my jar of Oaken's face cream and the book.

MARIE: I've been meaning to try that face cream! But what book?

ELSA: An old, old storybook, which our parents would read from when we were children.

ANNA: It's like a treasure for us.

MARIE: So, then you put on face cream and read stories?

ANNA: Nope! Then it was fort time!

ELSA: Anna collected all the cushions and pillows in the castle and brought them to the grand hall.

For Elsa!
With love from
your favorite sister!

When Elsa came back from giving gifts, the table was set for a royal feast. Anna showed her everything that had been made in her honor, saving the krumkake for last. When she saw it, Elsa was overjoyed, and Anna let out a hoot of happiness that the kids could hear in the village.

Then Elsa sat and opened presents, including yet another surprise from Anna—an Olaf-in-the-box! He makes an excellent gift, because he'll always make you laugh and never turns down a hug (especially if it's warm).

After Anna and Elsa helped take down the decorations, they were both exhausted. Just as the sisters were headed off to bed, a note arrived from one of the village girls. Elsa had succeeded in making it feel like everyone's birthday, not just her own.

The note was too cute not to share, so Elsa gave it to me to include here.

Dear Queen Elsa,

I love my new skates! I've never had anything new before. I get everything from my older sisters. Tomorrow, I'm going to start practicing for the Ice Games. When I'm old enough, I hope I can be on your team.

Thank you! Happy Birthday!

Marta

A Very Special and Delicious Recipe
Just for You from the Kitchen of Anna

Elsa's Favorite Krumkake

½ cup unsalted butter
1 cup white sugar
2 eggs
1 cup milk
1½ cups all-purpose flour
½ teaspoon vanilla extract
½ teaspoon butter flavoring, optional

Directions

Heat krumkake iron over the cooking fire.

Cream together the butter and sugar in a bowl.
Add the eggs, one at a time, and mix well using a
spoon. Pour in the milk, flour, vanilla, and butter
flavoring; mix well.

Place a teaspoon of the batter on the preheated
iron and press together. Cook until browned, about
30 seconds per side, depending on the heat.
Remove from the iron and quickly roll up around
a stick or around a cone before it hardens. Fill with
whipped cream if desired.

Makes 50 krumkake

ANNA: Then I made the most amazing pillow fort ever. It was *huge*. That's when Elsa added her special touches.

MARIE: Let me guess...ice?

ELSA: Of course! In keeping with classic Arendelle fort-making style.

ANNA: By the time she was finished, we had a mini version of her ice palace...just a bit comfier inside. Wasn't that when Olaf showed up?

MARIE: How is he at fort building?

ELSA: Not quite as impressive as he is at pick-up sticks. We played that as soon as he arrived.

ANNA: I think having twig arms gave him an advantage!

MARIE: Was it time for bed after pick-up sticks?

ELSA: No, it was "scary story" time. Anna told the tale of the Hairy Hooligan. Her impression would have made Olaf's hairs stand on end—if he had any.

ANNA: And then we *actually* heard it.

MARIE: Heard what?

ANNA: The Hooligan's cry! For real! WHOOOOOOOOARRRRRGGH!

Both girls were giggling at this point. I couldn't wait to hear why!

ELSA: It definitely sounded like it. We were quite worried! The noise was coming from outside. We slowly opened the castle doors, only to find...

ANNA: Sven! He couldn't sleep.

MARIE: So, the night turned into a slumber party?

ANNA: I guess it did.

ELSA: Complete with relaxation and facials. Olaf enjoyed Oaken's cream the most. What did he say...?

ANNA: He said, "I'm never taking this off. Just call it my new face!"

ELSA: He and Sven looked like brothers with the cream on.

MARIE: Sounds like fun.

ANNA: It was. But the best part of the night was listening to Elsa read from the storybook. She picked out one I love, *The Adventure of Princess Hildegard*.

ELSA: Yes, this is definitely my favorite memory from the year.

ANNA: Mine, too! I can't wait to make so many more with my favorite sister in the whole world!

ELSA: It helps that I'm your only sister!

Treat Yourself to the Magic
Oaken's Own **Night Cream**
Ingredients:

Arendelle glacier water
Crushed cloudberries
Oaken's secret beauty oil

Distilled sauna steam
Seaweed extract
Reindeer tears*

*harvested using laughter

**WARNING: MAY CAUSE
EXTREME BEAUTY**

An Arendelle Tradition: The Ice Games

In Arendelle, children toboggan before they can crawl, skate before they can walk, and learn to spell by carving their names into ice blocks! They take winter VERY seriously. Take this year's Ice Games, for instance!

Anyone with a team of three can enter the Games. This tradition started with the first ice harvesters, who lifted giant ice blocks that took three men to carry. Nowadays all are welcome—little kids or even grandparents who can barely hoist an ice cube.

Anna, Elsa, and Kristoff were very excited to enter this year. Would you believe Kristoff had never competed in the games? Kristoff—ice harvester to the bone.

Word of Elsa's magic had spread like a blizzard, and other competitors insisted she not use her powers. Elsa happily agreed and smiled when a team of Arendelle kids welcomed the competitors. "May the best team win," they piped. "Good luck!"

Elsa's event was ice carving. She grabbed her tools and went to work, sending up a flurry of snow. When the cloud settled, I thought Grand Pabbie and his clan had painted themselves blue and snuck in. It was Elsa's sculpture. First prize and without any magic!

Skating was next—Anna and Kristoff's event. Anna turned red. On the list of things she's bad at, skating is right after juggling plates. She slipped and fell twice before joining Kristoff on the ice.

But once they started, something magical happened. When Anna stumbled, Kristoff turned it into a move. If she hit a bump in the ice, he jumped with her. They made their accidents look like a routine, and came in second!

Tobogganing was last. All three teammates climbed onto the sled, Kristoff in the rear. Putting the heaviest person at the back keeps the front pointed up, so nobody gets a face full of snow!

Hold onto your hat, Kristoff!

Elsa, Anna, and Kristoff flew down the mountain. Elsa steered like a pro, always aiming the sled for the iciest, fastest snow. Suddenly, a second sled whipped by quicker than a snowball. They couldn't even make out the riders.

At the finish line, we saw who it was—the Arendelle kids! Their handmade sled was a genius design—soon available at Oaken's, I'll wager. Moments later Elsa, Anna, and Kristoff joined them, cheering.

Standing on the podium, Kristoff grinned wider than a fjord. He'd finally participated in the games—and even came in second! But everyone was proud to see the young winter superstars from Arendelle beaming victoriously.

I'm hoping I can come back next year just to enter. I'll be looking for teammates. If you want to join my team, just send me your details—carved in ice, of course!

Congratulations, everyone!

A Magical End to the Year

The darkest nights of winter bring the greatest spectacle: the northern lights. As the circle of seasons is completed, nature renews its magic for another year with a brilliant show in the sky.

Anna, Elsa, and many of us in Arendelle bundled up and climbed into the mountains, away from the shine of the village, for a chance to glimpse this wonder. This year, Kristoff brought his lute to sing a song in tribute. He barely got through the first verse before breaking off. I don't think he forgot the lyrics—the beauty struck him silent and made Sven sleepy.

NORTHERN LIGHTS BULLETIN

—Dear Citizens and Guests—

WANT TO SEE ONE OF NATURE'S GREATEST SHOWS?

WHEN IS THE BEST TIME?
IS IT...DARK? CAN'T SEE THEM IN THE DAYTIME!
IS IT...DRY? SNOW OBSCURES THE VIEW!
IS THE SKY...CLEAR? CLOUDS ARE AS BAD AS SNOW!

WHERE IS THE BEST PLACE?
GO OUTSIDE THE TOWN BECAUSE THE LAMPLIGHT
WILL SPOIL THE DISPLAY.
TAKE A SLEIGH RIDE INTO THE MOUNTAINS,
OR A BOAT RIDE ALONG THE COAST!

AND REMEMBER:
DRESS WARMLY—IT'S CHILLY OUT THERE!
KEEP LOOKING UP—IT MAY ONLY
LAST A FEW MINUTES.

HAVE A MAGICAL TIME!

The lights coiled and curled, like a giant living spirit, appearing and disappearing in gigantic shapes that made the moon look smaller than a pebble. Just after the lights peaked, Elsa and Anna were amazed when dozens of stars shone through in what looked like the shape of an enormous snowflake.

When they returned to the castle, Anna and Elsa felt inspired to commemorate the wonders of winter. They decided to exchange paper snowflakes written with words of appreciation to each other. Queen Elsa made this a new tradition, and it's something I will do with my family even after we leave Arendelle. I think it's the perfect way to end every magical year. Don't you?

I admire you,
Anna!

(you know who)

Love,
Elsa

Elsa & Anna,
You made this year
the best EVER!

From your
friend, Marie